THIS BOOK BELONGS TO

_____

The Adventures of

Bella & Harry

Let's Visit Rio de Janeiro!

Written by

Lisa Manzione

Illustrated by
Kristine Lucco

Bella & Harry, LLC

Dada ... dada! Da ... da!

"**Bella,** why are you singing and dancing in your bedroom, and trying on so many colorful outfits with feathers?"

6

"Well, Harry, our next family vacation is a visit to Rio de Janeiro, Brazil! We are going to the 'Carnival of Brazil' and will also learn to do the Samba (a Brazilian dance) while we are there. These outfits are Samba costumes."

8

"It is not that type of carnival, Harry. It is more of a celebration with parades, lots of good food, and lots of dancing!"

9

"Bella, why do the Brazilian people have such a big carnival?"

"The Carnival of Brazil is a celebration which takes place every year (usually in the month of February), just before Ash Wednesday. Ash Wednesday is a day that is celebrated forty-six days before Easter, an important day in the Christian religion."

"**Quickly,** start packing your bag! We don't want to be late for our airplane ride."

11

Now that we have arrived, our first stop is our hotel, which is in the barrio (or neighborhood) called Copacabana. It is just across the street from the famous Copacabana Beach!

"Let's put on our swimsuits, Harry!"

"I will race you to the coconut stand!"

"**Yummy,** Bella! I have never had fresh coconut milk before!"

"Yes, Harry, fresh coconut milk is a popular drink along this three-mile stretch of beach."

13

"**Let's** go, Harry! We are taking a cable car ride."

"Look at the amazing view from our glass cable car!"

"We can see the entire city of Rio de Janeiro as we head to the top of Sugarloaf Mountain."

"This is a cool looking mountain, Bella!"

14

"Yes, Harry, this is a monolithic granite and quartz mountain that rises straight from the water's edge."

"It's a what, Bella? I don't understand those fancy words!"

"Ha! Ha! That means it's a single, big rock."

"Well, why didn't you just say that, Bella?"

"**Harry,** let's make sure we stay with our family. We have to take two cable cars to reach the top of the mountain. This is our first stop, Urca Hill. The view of Guanabara Bay from here is magical!"

16

"**Let's** go, Harry. We are boarding the next cable car to get to the very top of Sugarloaf Mountain. From there, we will be able to see the entire city."

18

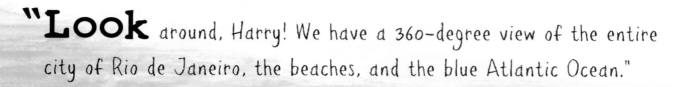

"**Look** around, Harry! We have a 360-degree view of the entire city of Rio de Janeiro, the beaches, and the blue Atlantic Ocean."

"Wow! This is a beautiful city!"

"**Come** on, Harry! We are heading back to the city for lunch."

"Let's look at our map so we know exactly where we are in South America."

Caribbean Sea

North Atlantic Ocean

Venezuela

Guyana

Suriname

French Guiana

Colombia

Ecuador

Peru

Brazil

Bolivia

Rio de Janeiro

Paraguay

South Pacific Ocean

Chile

South Atlantic Ocean

Argentina

Uruguay

"**Brazil** has a very tropical climate. Plus, it has one of the largest rivers in the entire world, the Amazon River."

"**Bella,** it was chilly when we left our home in the United States. Why is it so warm here in Rio de Janeiro?"

"Well, Harry, summer in Rio de Janeiro is during the months of December, January, February, and a portion of March. The average temperature during these months is about eighty degrees Fahrenheit. This is due to where Brazil is located in the world."

23

As Bella and Harry walked to lunch with their family, they passed through the Lapa barrio of Rio de Janeiro.

The famous "Selarón Steps", or "Escadaria Selarón", are located in Lapa. The steps were painted by an artist named Jorge Selarón and are very colorful.

"**We** are ready for our lunch. We are having 'Feijoada'. It is like a stew with black beans, cooked with pork or beef. We are also having 'Churrasco', which is several different types of roasted meats, usually served with salad and beans. For dessert, we are having 'Baba de Moca', which is an egg custard made with egg yolks, coconut milk, and sugar."

"Delicioso!"

Bella cried.

"What does that mean, Bella?"

"It means 'yummy'! Exactly what this food tastes like!"

"Delicioso! Delicioso!" Bella and Harry shouted.

"**Off** we go, Harry. We are boarding the cog train . . . next stop, 'Cristo Redentor'!"

"Wow!"

"Yes, Harry! WOW! That's the famous statue, 'Christ the Redeemer' or Cristo Redentor, in the Portuguese language."

29

"This statue is about 125 feet tall, including the base, or, about 125 cats stacked on top of each other. It is made of concrete and soapstone (a soft stone that feels like soap), and was built during the years 1922 to 1931. It is one of the most famous landmarks in Brazil, located at the top of Corcovado Mountain."

"**Bella,** we have seen some great sights in Rio de Janeiro. I love it here!"

"Me too, Harry, but it's time to head back to the hotel with our family."

31

Well, we had a great time with our family in Rio de Janeiro, Brazil and we hope you did too! For now, it is 'adeus', or good-bye in Portuguese, from Bella Boo and Harry too! See you on our next adventure!

Our Adventures in Rio de Janeiro

Harry getting ready to play soccer.

Bella and Harry dancing the Samba.

Bella relaxing on Ipanema Beach.

Harry zip lining through the Tijuca Forest.

Common Portuguese Words

yes – sim

no – náo

please – por favor

thank you (boy speaking) – obrigado

thank you (girl speaking) – obrigada

good morning – bom dia

good afternoon – boa tarde

good evening – boa noite

good-bye – adeus

hello – olá

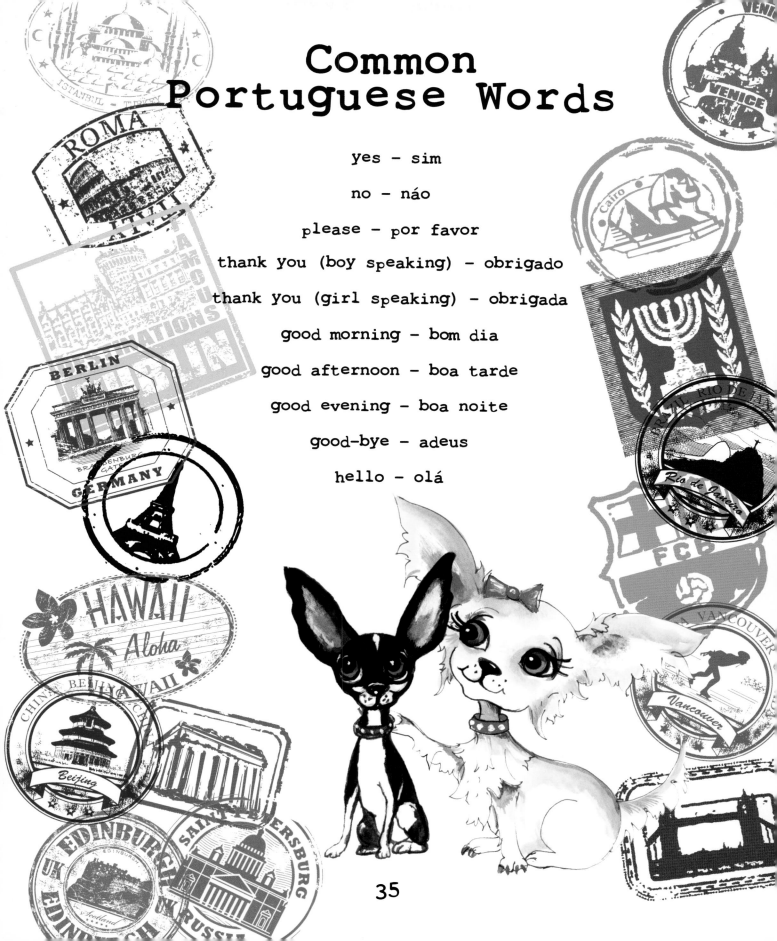

Library of Congress Cataloging-in-Publications Data is available
Manzione, Lisa
The Adventures of Bella & Harry: Let's Visit Rio de Janeiro!

ISBN: 978-1-937616-57-1
First Edition
Book Seventeen of Bella & Harry Series

For further information please visit:
BellaAndHarry.com
or
Email: BellaAndHarryGo@aol.com

Printed in the United States of America
Phoenix Color, Hagerstown, Maryland
August 2015
15 8 17 PC 1 1